10/20

ESCAPE GOAT

by **Ann Patchett**

illustrated by

Robin Preiss Glasser

HARPER

An Imprint of HarperCollinsPublishers

For the billy goats: Adriel, James, and Teddy
—A.P.

For Sasha and Ben. This and everything else.
—R.P.G.

Escape Goat
Text copyright © 2020 by Ann Patchett
Illustrations copyright © 2020 by Robin Preiss Glasser

Library of Congress Control Number: 2019937386
ISBN 978-0-06-288339-1

The artist used ink and watercolor to create the illustrations for this book.
Typography by Jeanne Hogle
20 21 22 23 24 SCP 10 9 8 7 6 5 4 3 2 1
❖
First Edition

Once there was a goat who lived in a pen on a farm.

He played hide-and-seek with the chickens on the other side of the fence.

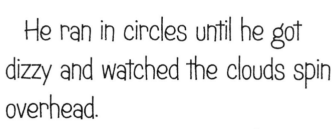

He ran in circles until he got dizzy and watched the clouds spin overhead.

He slept in a soft bed of hay (which made a great snack if he got hungry late at night).

"Good morning, goat!"

It was a perfectly nice life, but he was curious about the greater world, and so he decided to escape.

The goat went to see the horses and cows.

He ate a cabbage from the garden.

He scratched an itch on a pig's back because the pig couldn't reach it himself.

Mrs. Farmer was looking at the trampled petunias in her flower bed when she noticed the goat was missing.

"The goat's escaped!" she called.
Mr. Farmer, Uncle Nathan, and the three little Farmer children came running.

Mr. Farmer found the goat, led him back to the pen with a carrot, and shut the gate.

Mrs. Farmer said the goat had ruined her petunias.

In fact, Andrew and Archer Farmer had been
playing catch right over the flower bed.

The boys let the goat take the blame.

The next day, the goat went swimming with some ducks in the pond, napped in the sun, and ate four potatoes before Uncle Nathan noticed he was gone.

"Goat's escaped!" Uncle Nathan called.

When they found him, Andrew said the goat had eaten his homework,
even though he'd been looking for frogs all afternoon and hadn't done it.

Mr. Farmer raised the fence . . .

but not high enough.

Every day the goat escaped and every day Mr. Farmer brought him back. The goat didn't mind going back to his pen, and Mr. Farmer didn't mind making the fence higher. What Mr. Farmer *did* mind was all the mischief the goat caused when he was loose.

The goat kicked over a bucket of paint that Mrs. Farmer was using to paint the barn.

The goat ate all the cupcakes that had been made especially for Archer's birthday party.

And the goat stuck a wad of chewing gum to Mr. Farmer's chair. "Wait just a minute," Mr. Farmer said. "Goats don't chew gum."

"Escape Goat does," Andrew said.

"Excuse me," Nicolette called, but no one stopped to listen to her.

When finally the fence was too high to jump over, the goat lay down in the dirt, out of breath. That's when he realized it would be easy to scoot *under* the fence.

From there he rolled down the grassy hill and into the meadow.
Then he ran back to the top and rolled down again and again.
It was an incredible day!

Back at home, Uncle Nathan was making a pie and forgot to set the timer on the oven. He burned the pie, and it was so awful that he had to feed it to the pigs.

Uncle Nathan felt bad that there wasn't any pie for supper, so he said Escape Goat had eaten it.

Mr. Farmer shook his head. "Well," he said, "we're just going to have to keep the goat tied up all day. He can't keep running around making a mess out of everything." Mr. Farmer loved the goat, but he also loved pie and peace and quiet.

"EXCUSE ME!" shouted Nicolette.
"You're punishing the goat for things he didn't do," she said.

"But he stole the pie," said Uncle Nathan.

"And spilled the paint," said Mrs. Farmer.

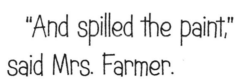

"And put gum on the chair," said Andrew.
"And ate the cupcakes," said Archer.

Mr. Farmer patted his daughter on the head. It was nice that she was sticking up for the goat, but the facts were the facts.

That was when Archer and Andrew started to wrestle over a ball and Andrew accidentally stepped on Archer's toe. Archer screamed.

"The goat stepped on Archer's foot!" Andrew said.

"See?" said Nicolette.
"The goat didn't do anything!!"

The goat was outside with a mouthful of alfalfa.

"I burned the pie," admitted Uncle Nathan.

"I left my gum on the chair," confessed Andrew.

"I spilled the paint," said Mrs. Farmer.

"I ate all the cupcakes," said Archer. "They were really good."

Everyone could agree that those things weren't the goat's fault.

That night, when Mr. Farmer tucked the goat into his bed of hay, he didn't shut the gate behind him.

Because, in the end, the goat always came home.